Bella at
the Ballet

Brian Ball

**Illustrated by
Hilda Offen**

PUFFIN BOOKS

PUFFIN BOOKS

Published by the Penguin Group
Penguin Books Ltd, 27 Wrights Lane, London W8 5TZ, England
Penguin Books USA Inc., 375 Hudson Street, New York, New York 10014, USA
Penguin Books Australia Ltd, Ringwood, Victoria, Australia
Penguin Books Canada Ltd, 10 Alcorn Avenue, Toronto, Ontario, Canada M4V 3B2
Penguin Books (NZ) Ltd, 182–190 Wairau Road, Auckland 10, New Zealand

Penguin Books Ltd, Registered Offices: Harmondsworth, Middlesex, England

First published by Hamish Hamilton 1990
Published in Puffin Books 1995
7 9 10 8 6

Printed in Hong Kong by Midas Printing Limited

J. 6
Bal

"Mum, I can dance like a real ballerina.
Look," said Bella.

She was in her new pink leotard.

She did a jump, and her baby brother
laughed at her.

"But you haven't had your first ballet
lesson yet, Bella," said Bella's mum.

"I will soon, Mum."

Her mum asked her if she had got
everything ready.

"Course!" said Bella.

Here were her new pink ballet shoes.
Here was her new pink bandeau. And she
was wearing her new pink leotard under
her dress.

"I'm all ready, Mum," said Bella.

"Good," said her mum, and she told
Bella to get Baby Tommy's push-chair.

"But he's only eighteen months old!"
said Bella. "Babies don't go to ballet
class. He'll want to join in, and he'll be
a pest."

Bella's mum said they couldn't leave
Tommy behind, so Bella grumbled all
the way to the bus-stop.

The bus came. *Wummmppp-wummmppp-woooosh!*

"Wummmppp-woooosh!" shouted Tommy. He liked the bus.

"Pest," hissed Bella.

"He's not," said her mum as they got on the bus. "Anyway, you used to do bus noises when you were a toddler."

"Where to today, Bella?" said the bus-driver. Bella smiled.

"Madame Vera's," she said. "I'm going to be a famous ballerina."

She showed him her new pink shoes and her new pink bandeau.

"What's that bandeau for?" he asked Bella.

Bella showed him. "It's to keep my hair up," she said.

The bus stopped at Madame Vera's.
Bella jumped down the steps and danced
inside. She waved to Dawn and James
who were in her class at school.

There were lots of other young children
with their parents, and some older
children too. Bella stopped dancing.
She was shy.
Tommy wasn't shy. He laughed and
shouted at the children.

12

"Pest!" hissed Bella.

Then Madame Vera saw her.

"Hello, Bella," she said. "You can be in the Beginners' Class with Dawn and James. Ready?"

The music started. It went la-*la*-la-*laa*.
So did Tommy: "Wa-*wa*-wa-*waaaaa!*"
"Shussshhh!" said Bella.
"Now, watch," said Madame Vera.
"Everybody!"

But Bella didn't watch Madame Vera and the other children, she watched Tommy.

Tommy was trying to dance too!

Bella was furious. She *knew* that Tommy would be a pest.

"Careful, Bella," said Madame Vera.

But Bella bumped into Dawn and they both fell over.

Tommy laughed. He thought it was a good game. He banged his feet up and down on the floor.

"Bella pushed me over, Madame
Vera!" wailed Dawn.

"Oh Bella didn't mean it, Dawn," said
Madame Vera. "Now, move gracefully,
like a swan."

17

Bella knew it was Tommy's fault. She glowered and glared at him until her mum told her not to be sulky.

"All right, Mum," said Bella.

The music started again. La-*la*-la-*laa*.
Bella tried to be graceful, like a swan.
She loved the music and the dancing.
Ballet was marvellous.

She smiled at her mum and at Madame
Vera. Wasn't she good at ballet?

Then her new pink bandeau slipped
down over her eyes.

Bella couldn't see very well. She
couldn't see a thing!

"Mum, it's gone dark," she said. "I
can't see."

Then she bumped into Dawn again
and Dawn went flying into the line of
mums and dads.

"Aaaaargh!" cried Dawn. "She's done it again."

Then Bella bumped into James.

"Aaaarrrgghh!" cried James. And he went flying too.

Tommy laughed and banged his feet and waved his hands in the air. He wanted to play, just like his sister.

"Oh dear," said Madame Vera. "That wasn't graceful, like a swan, Bella."

"No, it was like an elephant," said Dawn.

"She should be in a zoo, not a ballet class," said James.

Bella pushed the bandeau up. She didn't mean to be clumsy, and now she was furious with everyone. She saw James first.

"I'm good at ballet!" she cried. "You're not, James. Anyway, ballet is for girls, not boys."

Madame Vera tried not to laugh.

"Now, Bella," she said. "You're wrong. Ballet is for everyone. Boys are needed in ballet just as much as girls. Look at the bigger children," she said. "Over there."

Bella looked.

In the top class, the boys were lifting the girls.

"See?" said Madame Vera. "In real ballet, boys have to be strong enough to lift the girls."

But Bella was sulking.

"James is such a skinny little rabbit he couldn't lift Baby Tommy," she said.

Tommy heard his sister say "Tommy" and he laughed out loud again.

He laughed so much that all the children in Madame Vera's class had to laugh too. So did the mums and dads.

Then Bella felt ashamed of herself.
Here she was, sulking over nothing, and
Baby Tommy was happy and cheerful.
And she had been awful to him.

Tommy wasn't a pest. He was her little
brother, and he was lovely.

So Bella said she was sorry she had been miserable and she was sorry her bandeau had slipped and made her bump into James and Dawn.

"And you're not like a skinny rabbit," she told James.

James and Dawn then told her she wasn't really like an elephant.

"And you can be next to me again, if you like," they said. If she promised to be careful.

"Good," said Madame Vera. "Music!"

The music started, and the lesson was lovely, just as Bella knew it would be.

It was the same bus-driver on the way home.

"Did you like ballet, Bella? Are you going to be a famous ballerina?" said the bus-driver.

"Lovely!" said Bella. "And 'course I am! I can't wait till ballet next week."

Tommy laughed. He knew he would come too.

"Wooo-wummmppp!" he called, and off went the bus.